DISNEY's DOUG
Created by Jim Jinkins

The Funnie MYSTERIES

Invasion of the Judy Snatchers

by Dennis Garvey and Tommy Nichols

Illustrated by Bill Presing

Invasion of the Judy Snatchers is hand-illustrated by the same Grade A Quality Jumbo artists who bring you *Disney's Doug*, the television series.

DISNEY PRESS

New York

Original characters for "The Funnies" developed by
Jim Jinkins and Joe Aaron.

Copyright © 2000 by Disney Enterprises, Inc.

Printed in the United States of America.

1 3 5 7 9 10 8 6 4 2

The artwork for this book was prepared using pen and ink.

The text for this book is set in 13-point Leewood.

Library of Congress Catalog Card Number: 99-67850

ISBN 0-7868-4382-9

For more Disney Press fun, visit www.disneybooks.com

CONTENTS

INVASION OF THE JUDY SNATCHERS

"No, that's not your dentist! It's an alien! Run! Run!" cried Doug, bundled up on the couch watching a horror movie. One by one, Earth people were being replaced by imposter pod people.

Porchop was peeking at the movie from under Doug's blanket as Mom called from the kitchen, "Is everything okay, Douglas? That movie sounds awfully scary." Mom entered the living room, drying a plate with a dish towel.

Doug jumped up as the movie ended. "Well, the last kid on Earth was just taken over by the pod people. But I'm okay."

"That's nice, dear. Oh, Judy's home!" Mom exclaimed as the front door opened. "How was your rehearsal, dear?" she called to Judy.

Judy came into the den with a big, weird smile on her face. She saw the movie's credits rolling on the television. "Hi, Doug! Good movie? Hello, Porkchop, how are you?" she asked. Doug and Porkchop looked at each other and shrugged as Judy went over and kissed Mom tenderly on the cheek. Taking the plate and dish towel out of Mom's hands, Judy said, "Mother, you should get some rest. Why don't you sit down while I finish drying the dishes. And I'll make you a nice cup of tea. Can I get anything for you, Doug?"

"Uh . . . uh . . . no, thanks," stammered Doug, wondering what Judy was up to. "I'm going to bed." As he and Porkchop began to climb the stairs, he could hear Judy talking in the kitchen. "Hi, Dad. Tell me about your day."

Doug walked into his room and turned to Porkchop. "What do you think is going on?" Porkchop made an "I don't know" noise as Doug paced back and forth, trying to put all the pieces together. "It looked like Judy. It sounded like Judy. But, she was so . . . nice, pleasant, concerned with how we felt. Judy? Concerned with other people?"

Doug sat on his bed. "I think Judy has been taken over by the pod people. What do you think?" Porkchop shrugged.

After a moment, Doug said, "No, I'm probably still caught up in that movie. Maybe Judy's just happy. We didn't recognize it because she's never been happy before."

Doug slept fitfully, tossing and turning as scenes from the movie floated through his dreams. He woke up in the middle of the night with a start. "Get away from me, Pod Person!" he yelled, kicking his blanket off.

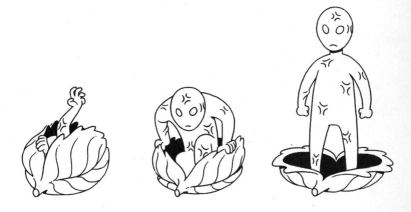

The next morning, Doug and Porkchop were shocked to see Judy washing dishes. When she saw Doug, she smiled and said, "Good morning, little brother! I've made you a nutritious break-fast, including some lovely apple fritters."

Doug and Porkchop froze, suspicious looks on their faces. "Who are you?" Doug asked. Man! he thought. What would his favorite detective, Smash Adams, do in this situation? He scanned the room for evidence: the O.J., the yogurt, the box of three-grain waffle mix, the bright smile on Judy's face. No empty pod, but she could have crumbled that up in the waffle mix. Doug wasn't fooled.

Judy laughed and said, "Now, you go ahead and eat while Porkchop and I play a quick game of squash in the park. Come on, Porkchop!" Caught completely off guard, Porkchop yipped, "Huh?" and went out with Judy, while Doug stood staring in shock. Since when did Judy care that Porkchop loved to play squash in the park?

Later that morning, Doug tried to talk to his parents about Judy. Pacing around the living room, he said, "I'm worried about Judy. She's been acting very strange. Have you noticed how . . . considerate she's been lately?"

Theda Funnie beamed. "She certainly has been a big help."

"Maybe you should think about helping a little more around the house, son," said Doug's father, as Judy glided into the room and picked up Dirtbike.

"I *am* helping out—by trying to prevent an alien invasion," Doug muttered under his breath.

"Mom, Dad, you both work so hard," Judy said. "Why don't I take little Cleopatra Dirtbike to the playground today? Babies need fresh air and sunshine. I don't have to be at rehearsal until after supper."

Dirtbike giggled as Theda beamed. "Oh, Judy, how sweet of you! Have fun."

"Would you like to come with us, Doug?" Judy turned to him with a smile. "You've been looking a little pale, you know."

"No, thanks," Doug said, and ran up the stairs with Porkchop right behind him. "We've got to *do* something about this!" he told his best nonhuman friend.

Sitting at his desk, Doug wrote neatly on the cover of a brand-new notebook, *Detective Log: Record of Unusual Behavior*. "Okay, Porkchop, now we know for sure that Judy has been taken over by a pod. It's up to us to stop the aliens from taking over Bluffington. We'll keep Judy under surveillance and make notes of everything she does in this detective's log."

Over the next few days, Doug filled page after page of the log with incidents of Judy's strange behavior: she made all the beds with special tucked-in corners, she ran the dishes through the dishwasher three timcs, and she constantly *smiled* at Doug and Porkchop.

As Doug walked home from school on Thursday afternoon, he had only one thought in mind: Pod Judy must be stopped!

Doug climbed the stairs and was headed for his room when Judy called him from her doorway. "Doug, there you are! Come on in."

Doug blinked at her. "But you said I'm not allowed to set foot in your room, even in cases of dire emergency."

"Nonsense!" Judy replied. "I've been waiting for you."

Doug looked into Judy's room and saw Porkchop dancing happily around with Judy while a jazz CD played. When

Porkchop saw Doug, he stopped dancing and grinned sheepishly.

Judy patted Porkchop and kept on dancing. "Come in, Doug. Join us. You're my brother. What's mine is yours. You're welcome in my room anytime."

As Doug entered Judy's bedroom, he noticed it was unusually neat and clean. A row of bandages and other medical supplies sat on top of her dresser. "Come on, Doug," she said. "What's wrong? Do you have a headache? Can I help?"

As Judy approached Doug, he noticed she was wearing a stethoscope. He backed away, yelling, "Stay away from me, whatever you are! You'll never get away with this. Bring back my sister right now! Or else!"

Doug ran to his room, Porkchop

following behind, and slammed the door. It was obvious that he couldn't fight this battle alone. From the evidence Doug had seen in Judy's room, it was clear that the aliens were planning medical experiments on Earthlings. He knew what he had to do. He picked up the phone. "Hello? It's me, Doug. Pod people are taking over Bluffington. Meet me at Swirly's in half an hour!"

Thirty minutes later, Doug sat in a booth at Swirly's with Al and Moo Sleech. Al said, "We've been expecting this. An attack by pod people is long overdue."

"Yes," agreed Moo. "It was clearly just a matter of time. You simply *must* defeat this alien, Doug Funnie. The future of our planet depends on you."

"Yes," Al continued. "If we're taken over

by the pod people, who'll be here when the *good* aliens arrive?"

Moo reached into his pocket and pulled out a vial of what looked like dirt. Doug took the vial and turned it over in his hand. "Looks like dirt," he deduced.

Moo laughed. "Dirt! Oh, that's rich! What you hold in your hand, Doug Funnie, is soil. Grade A, slightly wormy, planet Earth soil. Thrown, it will send any alien scrambling back to the mothership."

Al nodded. "Drastic as it sounds, I believe my brother is correct. Just throw it at the alien's body, not the face, of course. But keep in mind, the element of surprise is essential. The alien must not see the soil coming, or it will take evasive action. Aliens simply cannot tolerate soil."

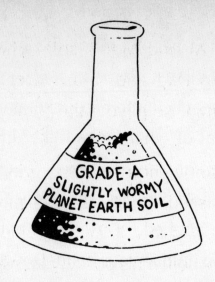

GRADE-A
SLIGHTLY WORMY
PLANET EARTH SOIL

Doug stared at the vial of soil doubtfully. "I don't know," he said. "The real Judy would kill me if I threw dirt at her."

Al nodded. "And that's exactly how you'll know that your sister is back!"

Doug kept the soil in his pocket as he ate dinner that evening with the family (Judy had spent the afternoon making vitamin-enriched beet lasagna). Doug was wondering if it was really a good idea to fling Al and Moo's soil, when Judy turned to Dad and said, "After dinner, Dad, can I help you tie some fishing flies?"

Pleasantly surprised, Dad grinned, but Doug gasped. This was too much! He knew he had to act, and fast! He felt for the vial of soil in his pocket and nodded to Porkchop. "Excuse me," he said, getting up from the table. "I've got to go upstairs to work on a project."

"Let me know if you need any help," Judy said. Doug ran upstairs at top speed. He just had to think of a way to use the Sleech weapon on Pod Judy without getting killed by either Judy.

Later that night, he still hadn't come up with a really good plan to save Planet

Earth from the aliens, so he decided to sleep on it.

Friday evening, Doug came home for supper to find Judy was gone. "Where's Judy?" he asked his mother.

"Oh, have you forgotten, dear?" Mom answered. "Tonight is Judy's school play. She's going to be Florence Nightingale. Aren't you coming?"

Doug thought for a second. With everybody out, he'd have the house to himself and the whole evening to plan his attack on Pod Judy. "I can't, Mom," he said. "I have to finish my project."

And save the Earth, he thought to himself.

Doug and Porkchop entered Judy's

spotless room and hid in the closet. It wouldn't be long now. With the vial of soil in his hand, he waited for Judy to come home.

When Judy finally entered the room, Doug was focusing so hard on his mission that he didn't notice her dropping her jacket and purse on the floor. She finished

the banana she was eating and tossed the peel, missing the wastebasket as she stretched out on her bed with her shoes still on.

"Aha!" Doug cried as he sprang out of the closet.

Judy jumped up and screeched, "How dare you enter my room without permission? How dare you enter my room, *period*!"

Doug blew a handful of soil right at Judy. "Your game is up, Pod Person!" he shouted.

Judy bellowed, "Have you lost your mind, you . . . you dirt-throwing knave? I will destroy you!"

"Judy, it's you! You're back!" Doug cried as he and Porkchop exchanged high fives. "Your body was taken over by pod people from outer space. You were being nice, kind, and considerate. You made three-grain waffles, you cleaned the house for no reason, you told Mom and Dad they needed more rest, you welcomed me into your room, you had bandages and surgical supplies for alien experiments in plain sight, *and* you haven't yelled at me in five days. Aw man, Judy, can't you see? The evidence speaks for itself. But now the nightmare is over. I saved you!"

Judy glared at Doug. "I was in *character*,

Dougie! I played the famous nurse Florence Nightingale in tonight's play, and I needed to capture her kind, compassionate nature. You should be applauding me, not throwing dirt in my face."

Doug stammered, "Gee, Judy, I'm sorry. I was only trying to rescue you. You should have told me you were just rehearsing!"

Judy stalked out the door, pausing to tell Doug, "You'd better clean up the dirt, Dougie. And be gone when I get back. I have another role to prepare for next month's play."

Doug and Porkchop exchanged looks. "Oh," Doug said, "what play is that?"

"*Cinderella*!" Judy barked. "And I'm playing her stepmother. Now, clean up that mess!" Taking a dustpan and broom

from the closet, she thrust them at Doug. "And, no!" she concluded dramatically at the doorway. "You *can't* go to the ball!"

As Judy stomped down the stairs, Doug began sweeping up the dirt, happy that Judy was not a pod person and determined to stay out of her way for the next month.

THE CASE OF THE SHRINKING HAT

Doug stood looking at himself in the mirror. He was wearing a straw cowboy hat with a wide brim. "What do you think of my new hat, Porkchop?"

Porkchop made an approving noise and sat up on Doug's bed, watching as Doug continued to model the hat, striking cowboylike poses. "It's for the Annual Bumpkin Day Hoedown next week," said Doug. "I reckon I'll be the best darn-tootin' cowboy little Miss Mayonnaise has ever seen!" he declared in a cowboy voice.

Doug grabbed Porkchop's paw and

started dancing around his room, singing out square-dance calls. "Allemande left, and do-si-do! Swing your partner and away you go! Oops!" Doug caught his foot under the leg of a chair and went flying across the room, sending Porkchop in a slam dunk back onto the bed.

"Sorry about that, Porkchop," muttered Doug, as he picked himself up off the floor. He put his hat back on the windowsill. "I guess I need a little more practice before I'll be ready for that square dance."

Porkchop nodded sympathetically as they headed downstairs for supper.

The next afternoon, when Doug came home from school, Porkchop was waiting outside the house, watching a mother robin sitting in a nest with her baby birds. "Hey, Porkchop," Doug called. "Ready for some square-dance lessons? I got this CD from the library that has all the instructions. Come on, man. You gotta help me get ready to dance with Patti!"

Porkchop gave a "why fight it?" shrug and quickly tied a red bandanna around his neck as he followed Doug upstairs.

Doug started the CD and put on his straw hat. "Hmmm," he said, "that's funny. The brim looks smaller than it did yesterday. Could it be . . . shrinking?"

As the square-dance caller shouted out commands, Doug continued, "What could make it shrink, Porkchop?" But Porkchop had thrown himself into the dance, clapping his

paws and yelping in perfect time to the music. As Doug struggled to keep from falling, Porkchop expertly executed every last promenade and do-si-do, sashaying all around the room and ending with a big flourish and a bark that sounded a lot like "Yee haw!"

Doug, having landed on the floor once again, stared up at Porkchop in amazement. Porkchop shrugged and offered a paw to help him up. "Oh well, you do the dancing, I'll do the detective work," Doug said.

The next morning, while putting on his vest to go to school, Doug glanced at his straw hat on the windowsill. "Porkchop!" Doug said. "Look at my hat! It was much bigger than this last night. There's something very funny going on here.

"I don't know how," Doug went on, "but we're gonna get to the bottom of it."

Porkchop barked his agreement. Doug put the hat back on the windowsill and turned to Porkchop. "I'm leaving you in charge while I'm at school,"

Doug announced. "Don't let that hat out of your sight. If it starts shrinking, make it stop!"

Porkchop snapped to attention and saluted as Doug left the room. Then he sat on the bed to keep watch. Porkchop imagined how pleased Doug would be when he came home to find the hat had not shrunk. He pictured himself marching proudly up onto a stage, where Doug placed a medal around his neck. "Good work, Porkchop! You're the World's Greatest Watchdog Detective!"

Hearing the shouts of the adoring crowd, Porkchop contentedly curled up on the bed and fell into a deep sleep. For some reason, he kept dreaming that birds surrounded him, chirping loudly.

Doug raced home after school, anxious to see if Porkchop had kept the hat from shrinking any more. Entering his room, he found Porkchop sleeping soundly on his bed. "Porkchop!" Doug cried, as Porkchop slowly woke up and stretched lazily. "You were supposed to watch the hat!"

Doug picked up the hat, which had gotten even tinier during the day. "Did you see or hear *anything*? Footsteps? Eerie laughter?

The sound of shrinking straw?" Porkchop shrugged his shoulders apologetically and made an *uh-uh* sound.

That night, as Doug went to sleep, Porkchop sat at the foot of the bed, staring at the hat. After his long afternoon nap, he was now wide-awake and fully alert for a long night of surveillance. And he was determined to make up for his lapse.

Porkchop watched the hat all night, but nothing happened. He tried to figure out what could be causing the hat to shrink. In his imagination, he saw Doug putting on the hat, which now was so small, it barely covered Doug's head. Suddenly Porkchop realized that the hat wasn't shrinking at all. Doug's head was getting bigger! Porkchop watched in amazement as Doug's head grew and grew, until it couldn't fit in the room. Porkchop shook himself out of his fantasy to stare at the hat again.

Just as the sun was coming up through the window, Porkchop rubbed his eyes with his paws and yawned. Then he curled up next to Doug, ready to catch a quick nap.

Suddenly, he heard a bird chirping very loudly.

What could be behind the incredible shrinking hat?

Porkchop covered his ears with his paws for a few seconds and then opened his eyes wide. That chirping sounded like it was right next to him! It was. He looked

just in time to see the culprit pulling straw from the hat and flying away.

Porchop poked Doug with his paw. "What is it, Porkchop?" asked Doug groggily. Porkchop pointed excitedly to the hat on the windowsill.

The mother robin was pulling more straw from what was left of the hat. As the bird flew away, Doug and Porkchop ran to the window and watched. The robin added the straw to the side of a nest, where four baby robins watched their mother work.

Doug smiled. "That's why the hat kept getting smaller! You solved the case, Porkchop."

Porkchop beamed with pride, as Doug took the hat and sailed it out the window so it landed in the branch under the robin's nest. "There! She can get at it easier now. I can get another straw hat for the dance. Right, Porkchop?"

Porkchop yelped in agreement and opened Doug's dresser drawer. Doug laughed. "You're right, I'd better birdproof the next hat. I'll keep it out of sight!"

THE MYSTERY MEAT MYSTERY

"Man, what *is* this stuff?" Doug held up an oddly shaped piece of brownish-grayish-purplish meat dripping in lumpy gravy.

Skeeter and Patti, sitting at the cafeteria table with Doug, laughed. "The menu *says* it's Saucy Meat Surprise," Skeeter replied doubtfully.

"Yeah," said Patti, poking at the food on her plate. "But what kind of meat? It looks just like the meat in yesterday's Meatball Perplexity."

"Yeah, and I think we had it in the Flaming Meat Wonders the day before that," Skeeter added.

Doug peered at the meat again. He was getting suspicious. He had never seen any meat outside the school cafeteria that looked like this stuff. "Hmmm, it even looks the same as last week's Spicy Cutlet Enigmas. I'm beginning to see why everybody calls it mystery meat."

Skeeter honked. "It's always been a mystery to me."

"You know what?" Doug said. "I'll bet it's all the same stuff, just disguised with different gravy and sauces!"

"Or maybe it's not even meat at all," Patti replied. "Maybe it's just some kind of tofu or soybean experiment. *Or* it might even be spicy cardboard."

Skeeter gasped. "Wow!" he said, excitedly. "We could be vegetarians and we don't even know it!"

Just then, the bell rang. As everybody began to head for afternoon classes, Patti stood and said, "The real mystery is why we're eating something if we don't know what it is." She walked over to Flo, the cafeteria lady. Doug and Skeeter followed her.

"Excuse me," Patti said politely. "Could you please tell me what kind of meat is used in these meat patties?"

Flo scowled at Patti and yelled, "It's meat. Cooked meat." She turned, muttering to herself, "It *is* meat. It's good meat. It's what's for lunch." She hurried into the kitchen, still muttering.

Patti turned to Doug and Skeeter. "She's acting awfully funny," Patti said. "There's something weird going on here."

Doug agreed. "You're right, Patti. We should get to the bottom of this."

Skeeter jumped up. "I guess that means

the Dumpster, right? Last one in is a rotten egg!"

Patti wrinkled her nose. "Ewwww, the Dumpster? I don't think we have to climb around in garbage. We'll find the answer by doing some good old-fashioned detective work."

"Yeah, like good old-fashioned detectives!" Doug said.

For a moment, Doug imagined himself and Patti as Sherlock Holmes and Dr. Watson. "So you see, Dr. Mayonnaise," Doug said, looking at a piece of meat through his magnifying glass, "it's elementary."

Patti threw down her magnifying glass. "Ooh, Doug, you're so . . . sleuth-y!" She reached out and put her arms around him. Suddenly, Doug felt the real Patti shaking him by the shoulders.

"Come on, Doug, we'll be late for class," Patti said, as Doug came out of his fantasy. He hurried after Patti and Skeeter.

"We can start our investigation right after school today," he called to his friends.

That afternoon, when classes were over, Doug, Patti, and Skeeter slipped into the now deserted cafeteria. "Okay," Doug whispered. "Let's head into the kitchen and split up. Patti, you check the pantries, I'll check the refrigerator, and Skeeter, you can look in the garbage cans. Are you all set?"

Skeeter whispered back, "Cool, man, but there's lots more garbage to choose from in the Dumpster."

As they entered the kitchen, Doug found that the refrigerators had chains with huge padlocks on them. Each refrigerator door had a large sign on it that said, **KEEP OUT! THIS MEANS YOU! AND YOU TOO!** Under that in smaller, bold letters it read **USE CAUTION: SLIPPERY WHEN WET.**

Patti reported back that the pantries

were also double-locked and had signs saying **PROTECTIVE HEADGEAR MUST BE WORN AT ALL TIMES!** plastered all over the doors. Hearing a muffled sound from the cafeteria, Doug and Patti froze. Silently moving along the kitchen wall, they inched toward the door. When they looked out, they saw that Skeeter had gotten stuck upside down in a garbage can.

"Skeeter, you scared us! What happened?" asked Patti.

As Doug helped him out of the can, Skeeter said, "I told you we should check

the Dumpster. There's lots more room to move around in there. Besides, these cans have already been emptied."

Patti replied, "Everything in the kitchen is locked up. Why would you have to lock up food?"

"I don't know," said Doug. "Unless it could . . . get loose." He snapped his fingers. "I've got it. Let's come back here early tomorrow morning. We can see the food being delivered. Then we'll find out what it really is."

Patti and Skeeter agreed, and the three of them headed out the cafeteria door.

At seven sharp the next morning, Doug, Patti, and Skeeter were hiding in the bushes behind the school. They were waiting for the food-service delivery truck. When the truck pulled up, Skeeter stared through his binoculars while Doug and Patti peered out of the bushes. Two delivery men wearing dark glasses jumped out of the truck and looked around before opening its back doors.

"What's that box they're unloading, Skeet?" Doug asked.

Focusing the binoculars, Skeeter honked, "Ticky Tacky Taco Company. One hundred shells. Hey, I'll bet we're having tacos for lunch today."

"Tacos full of mystery meat," said Patti.

"Yeah, keep watching, Skeeter, they're

bound to bring the meat out soon. Those big cans they're carrying! What do they say?" Doug asked urgently.

Skeeter looked through the binoculars. "Oh, no!" he cried. "It's worse than we thought. Aaagghhhh! Giant horseflies!"

Doug gasped, "They're making us eat horseflies? Let me see that." Doug took the binoculars and looked through them. Then he looked at the front of the binoculars. A horsefly was sitting on one of the lenses. As the horsefly flew away, Doug said, "There was a horsefly on the binoculars, Skeeter. Did you see what the label on the cans said?"

"No, man, all I saw—oh, no! The truck's pulling away. We missed it!"

Doug frowned. "We have to get a closer look. Come on!" As Doug, Patti,

and Skeeter tiptoed into the cafeteria, they could
hear sounds from the kitchen. "They must be making lunch now," said Patti. "We have to try to see into there, but the windows in the kitchen door are too high!"

Skeeter suddenly brightened. "I've got it! The garbage can!"

Skeeter positioned the garbage can in front of the door and climbed up, balancing his feet on the edges of the can. Peering through the window, he said excitedly, "Flo's spooning meat from a big can into the taco shells. I can't read what the can says. We need to get closer. If only we could think of some kind of a diversion . . . Aaaaaah!"

Skeeter lost his balance and fell into the garbage can, which began to roll noisily across the floor. As Flo rushed out to check on the commotion, Doug and Patti slipped through the swinging door into the kitchen. They ran breathlessly over to the can of meat and turned it around.

"Oh, no!" cried Patti. "I can't believe it!"

"It can't be true," said Doug. "But it is!"

Doug and Patti stared at the label, which was blank except for a large red question mark and the words MYSTERY MEAT INC. "It *is* Mystery Meat!" Patti and Doug said at the same time.

Doug sat down on a nearby chair. "They use the same meat in everything from hamburgers to Cajun Meat Teriyaki," he said.

"They keep the pantries locked up like Fort Knox. Are they afraid of us getting in or of something getting out? And why do they need protective headgear? Just what are they protecting their heads from? The meat is delivered in an unmarked truck driven by men in dark glasses—"

"And what is that burping sound coming from . . . the refrigerator?" asked Patti.

They looked at each other, both deciding exactly the same thing. Some mysteries are better left unsolved.

RUNAWAY MOM

"Hey, Mom, I'm home!" Doug called as he came in from school one spring afternoon. The house was quiet and it seemed like nobody was there. Doug went into the kitchen to make himself a snack.

He noticed a stack of Theda and Phil's old high school yearbooks and a letter on the counter beside the refrigerator. As he moved the books aside to make room to prepare a sandwich, the envelope fell to the floor and the letter slipped out. Bending down to pick it up, Doug couldn't help reading the first line.

"Dear Phil," the letter began. "So long.

I'm going away. It's hard to imagine even a day without you, but I have no choice. I won't forget you. Love, Theda."

"So long? I won't forget you? Oh, no!" cried Doug. "Mom's leaving home!" Racing from the kitchen, he ran upstairs to his room. He noticed that the attic stairs were pulled down, and stacks of old magazines and photo albums were piled in the hallway. When he looked into the attic, he saw his mother opening an old trunk. "Oh, no! She wants to take everything with her," he said.

Doug ducked into his room. "I'm not too late. She's not gone yet. She's packing. I can still stop her. But how?" Doug asked himself.

Looking out the window, he saw Judy coming home. He raced downstairs to meet her, with the letter in his hand.

"Judy, we've got a big problem," Doug whispered loudly as he pulled her into the living room.

"What is the panic, little brother?" asked Judy, pulling herself free from Doug's grasp. "It must be serious for you to risk your life by violating my personal space like this."

Doug held up the letter. "It *is* serious, Judy," he said, solemnly. "Look at this!"

Judy's eyes widened as she read the letter. "So that's why Mom brought home a lot of cardboard boxes!"

Doug slapped his forehead. "Of course!" he cried. "She's planning to move out!"

Judy was so upset that she fell back onto the couch. "Oh, no! What will we do?" she cried. "We have to tell Dad."

"I wonder if Dad's already read the letter," Doug said.

"Poor Dad! He'll be devastated," Judy moaned.

"I can't believe Mom wants to leave us," Doug said. "We just got cable."

"Don't be silly," Judy replied disdainfully.

"She can get cable at her new house."

"Maybe we can stop her," Doug suggested. "She's upstairs in the attic now, packing a trunk."

Judy jumped up off the sofa. "That's it! We'll stop her! Good thinking, little brother. All these years of exposure to me have finally rubbed off. Where's Cleopatra?"

"You mean Dirtbike. She's sleeping in her crib," Doug replied.

"Good!" Judy exclaimed. "Mom won't leave without saying good-bye to the baby. Let's hurry! We haven't much time!"

A little while later, Doug and Judy sat nervously in the living room with Dirtbike and Porkchop, trying to act as though nothing were wrong. When Theda came down from the attic, dragging the trunk, she smiled and said, "Oh, here you all are. Could you help me put this stuff in the car?"

Unbelievable! Doug thought. Mom actually wanted them to help her leave.

Theda went to the ring where her car keys normally hung. "That's odd," she said, puzzled. "What have I done with my keys?" Doug and Judy exchanged glances as Theda walked to the door. "Maybe I left them in the car."

As Theda went outside, Doug said, "Judy, this will only work if we don't break our cover. As long as she doesn't suspect we know her secret plan, we're set."

"Yes, if we can stall Mom until Dad gets home, he'll fix everything," Judy said. "Quiet, here she comes!"

Theda entered the house with a perplexed look. "Oh, dear," she said. "Someone has broken into my car and taken the steering wheel! And I still can't find my keys."

Judy walked over to Theda and put a hand on her shoulder. "We'll call the police and report the robbery, Mother," she said. "You keep looking for your keys."

Doug picked up the phone and pretended to dial the police the way he'd seen detectives do in movies. "Hello?" he said into the phone. "This is Doug Funnie at 21 Jumbo Street, Bluffington. I'd like to report a robbery. Yes. Grand theft, auto. Well, part of the auto. The steering wheel, to be exact."

Theda walked upstairs, shaking her head saying, "Perhaps I left them in my jacket pocket."

The second she was gone, Doug slammed the phone down. Judy ran over to the sofa. She pulled out Dirtbike's sweater and hat from under a cushion and dressed the baby hurriedly. "Good," said Doug. "I'll get lost for a while with Dirtbike. That ought to give us enough time till Dad gets home."

Judy plunked Dirtbike into her stroller and wheeled her toward the front door, pulling Doug along. Just then, Theda came down the stairs.

"Judith? Douglas?" Theda said, sternly. "Before you leave, I'd like to know what's going on here."

"Why, Mother," Judy said, innocently. "Whatever do you mean? Doug's just taking the baby out for an innocent stroll."

"Well, when I opened my closet to look for my keys, I discovered that all of my shoes are missing. Do you know anything about that?"

Doug and Judy tried to look amazed. "Um . . . uh . . . ," Doug stammered.

"Well, where did you last see them?" Judy asked.

"All right, you two," Theda said. "No more nonsense. What is going on?"

"We're sorry, Mom," Doug said. "We just wanted to stop you from leaving."

"Leaving?" Theda asked. "To go to Déjà Vu? I'm coming right back."

"Don't try to deny it, Mom," Doug said. "We know the truth. You left a letter out on the kitchen table for Dad. The letter said you're leaving. You've been packing boxes all day. You packed your trunk and pulled it out of the attic. You even asked Judy and me to help you load the car for your getaway. Mom, how could you?"

Theda stared at Doug and Judy with her mouth agape.

"Oh, children!" Theda laughed. "This letter is over twenty years old. I wrote it to your father when we were teenagers and I was going to camp for the summer! Do you think I still write with purple marker on rainbow stationery?"

Doug looked relieved. "Then you're not leaving?"

"Oh, Douglas." Theda smiled, giving him a hug. "How could you ever think I would leave you all? This family means everything to me."

"Then it was all just a misunderstanding," Judy said, "which never would have happened if you hadn't jumped to conclusions, Dougie." Judy pointed her finger at Doug.

"Oh, sure, blame it all on me!" Doug fumed. "Whose idea was it to hide the shoes? And the keys? Huh?"

"Who removed the steering wheel?" Judy asked.

"Now, how could I ever think of leaving such a happy family?" Theda said, laughing.

Doug and Judy looked at each other, and then they both burst out laughing, too.

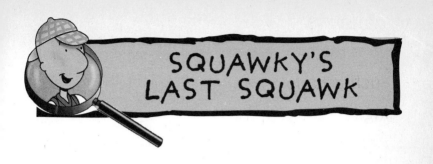

The bell rang for lunch, and the doors of each classroom flew open. Kids streamed into the hallways, raced to their lockers, dropped off their books, and headed for the cafeteria. As Doug and Patti walked along the hall with a group of their friends, Roger bumped into Doug.

"Hey! Watch it, Funnie!" Roger barked. "I've got a lunch date at Chez Honque. Enjoy your cafeteria grub, suckers!" Roger exited the school quickly, carrying his backpack in front of him as he raced out to his limo in the parking lot.

"Great," Doug said. "Roger's eating filet mignon while we have mystery meat."

Meanwhile, Ms. Kristal made her way to the storage room, where she kept her parrot, Squawky, when he wasn't in the classroom. She often brought Squawky to school to help with her dramatic presentations.

"Hello there, Squawky! Mommy's here!" Ms. Kristal called out as she switched on the light. "I've got some delicious sunflower seeds for your lunch today." She pulled the cover off the cage, and to her horror she discovered that Squawky was not there. Nothing remained except his still-swinging perch and a few stray feathers.

"Help! Help!" Ms. Kristal cried.

77

"Squawky's been birdnapped!" She ran upstairs, holding the empty cage, and burst into Principal Bob White's office without knocking.

Dropping the empty cage with a bang, she startled Principal White, who was busily arranging his toupee. "Oh where, oh where has my little bird gone?" she sobbed.

Embarrassed, Principal White dropped his comb and crammed his toupee back on his head. "Oh where, oh where can he be?" he sang back. "If I'm reelected Mayor, I promise you I'll find your bird—"

Ms. Kristal interrupted, "I know I locked the cage this morning after Squawky helped me read *Peter Pan* to the class. He gave a heartrending performance as Tinker Bell. Then Doug Funnie took him down to the storage room."

"Doug Funnie!" exclaimed Principal White. "We have our culprit. Another case solved by Bob 'Crimebuster' White!"

"Oh, no," Ms. Kristal replied. "Doug would never do anything like that."

Principal White took Ms. Kristal by the elbow and walked her to the door.

"Have no fear, good teacher-person," he said. "With Bob White on the job, parrots can sit easily on their perches. Vote for me!" Ignoring Ms. Kristal's protests, he nudged her out the door and threw both arms in the air, making victory signs.

Doug, Patti, Skeeter, Beebe, and Connie were all sitting at the lunch table together, buzzing about the news that Squawky had disappeared.

"Who would even *want* to take that noisy bird," Beebe muttered, as she took a bite of her pizza. "He makes such a racket. And he kicks seeds on the floor. And his performance as Tinker Bell stank."

"Well, maybe somebody really needed a bird that could recite passages from famous books," Patti responded. "He sure has made Ms. Kristal's literature class a lot more fun."

Doug cleared his throat. "Whoever did it must have left some clues behind," he said. "If we examine the evidence, it's sure to lead us to the birdnapper."

"Attention. Attention." Doug was interrupted by the school intercom. "This is your mayor—I mean principal—speaking. There's been a birdnapping. I don't want to name names, but could I see Douglas Funnie in my office right now . . . and bring the bird you stole." The kids gasped, and all eyes were on Doug. "Vote for me," Principal White concluded.

"Huh?" Doug looked up, bewildered. "Me? He thinks I took Squawky. He must not be looking at the evidence right."

Roger entered the cafeteria and called out to Doug, "Hey, Funnie, what'd you do with the bird? I guess you needed a mascot for the Doofus Squad, right?" Everyone stared at Doug.

Connie thought for a moment, then her eyes widened. "You *were* the last person to see Squawky," Connie stated suspiciously. "After all, *you* took him back to the storage room this morning."

"Oh come on, you guys. You can't really think I'd steal Squawky. Squawky and I were like brothers, except he was a bird. I cracked seeds for him. I changed his paper. I even helped him run lines for his role in *Treasure Island* . . . well, he only had to squawk a couple of times, but I helped him!" Doug stood up determinedly and marched to the principal's office.

"I believe you, Doug," Patti called out after him as he went through the cafeteria door.

"Me, too, man," Skeeter piped up.

"I hope Ms. Kristal believes me," Doug said to himself.

Later that afternoon, Doug joined Patti in her booth at Swirly's, where she was sipping a Frothy Goat. "Ms. Kristal is really upset," Doug told her. "She doesn't think I took Squawky, but there doesn't seem to be another explanation. Principal White says he's keeping an eye on me because he knows I did it. Oh, man," Doug said, bummed. "I've got to find out what really happened to Squawky."

"I'll help you, Doug," Patti said. "Let's take a walk and think this through." Patti got up and they went outside. As they walked along the street, she said, "You took Squawky down to the storage room right before lunch."

"And Ms. Kristal discovered him missing right after the lunch bell rang," Doug added.

Patti continued, "So whoever took him had to have done it at the very beginning of lunch period."

Doug paused beside Patti and said, "So who was missing at lunchtime?"

"Hmmm," Patti murmured, deep in thought.

The next day, Ms. Kristal attempted to act like business as usual. She was dressed in a pirate's costume, playing Long John Silver in *Treasure Island*, but her heart wasn't really in it.

In fact, Ms. Kristal seemed so sad and distracted, everyone was relieved when the

bell finally rang. Roger threw his backpack over his shoulder and charged down the aisle, bumping into Skeeter as he raced out of the room.

Doug and Patti stood at Ms. Kristal's desk. "Don't worry, Ms. Kristal," Doug told her. "Patti and I will find Squawky."

Ms. Kristal nodded and tried to smile, but her eyes filled with tears. "I hope so,

Doug," she replied. "I keep thinking of his empty cage. I wonder why they didn't take it. What did they use to carry him out of school?"

Doug stroked his chin thoughtfully. "Yeah, what *did* they carry him out in?" he wondered.

After eating lunch quickly, Doug and Patti headed for the storage room to look for clues. As they turned on the light, they saw that Ms. Kristal had put Squawky's cage back in its usual place and covered it. Doug noticed a couple of small feathers on the floor. He bent to pick them up, but Patti stopped him. "Wait, Doug! Use these," she whispered, pulling a pair of rubber gloves from her pocket. "We don't want to mess up any fingerprints."

As Doug started to put on the gloves, his elbow bumped the cage. "Awk," they heard from within the cage. "Shiver me timbers! Awk!"

Patti jerked the cover off the birdcage. "Squawky!" they both gasped. "You're back!" Most of the kids had finished lunch when Doug and Patti came flying into the cafeteria, carrying Squawky's cage between them. They spotted Ms. Kristal at the teachers' table and shouted to her. "Ms. Kristal! Squawky's back!"

Ms. Kristal leaped up and raced over to Doug and Patti, as all the kids gathered around them. "Oh, my Squawky!" Ms. Kristal cried, as she quickly opened his cage and pulled him into her arms. "Where have you been?"

"Yes, that *is* the question, isn't it," Doug said thoughtfully. As he eyed the other kids, he realized that many of them were looking at him suspiciously. Roger had walked in a moment earlier and was standing next to Patti. "Well, you know," Roger whispered loudly, "Funnie *was* the last one seen with Squawky . . ." The kids all murmured.

Patti, frowning thoughtfully, looked directly at Roger. She said slowly, "Roger, when did you get here?"

"What do you mean?" said Roger, shifting uneasily back and forth. "I was here all along."

"But you weren't in the cafeteria at the beginning of lunch period," Doug pointed out. "Come to think of it, you weren't here for lunch the day Squawky disappeared, either."

Roger spoke nervously. "Hey, I had a lunch date."

Doug continued. "I remember something else about that day. You left the cafeteria in a big hurry. You were carrying your backpack in front of you, as if you had something special in it. You knew I took Squawky to the storage room after class. And you were the first one to try to put the blame on me. Now you're late for lunch today, the day Squawky was returned."

Roger scowled. "What are you two, a couple of detectives? Does everybody suddenly have to know everything about me?"

Squawky suddenly spoke up from his swinging perch. "Awk! Roger! Get your jammies on and give Mommy a beddy-bye kiss!" The kids all burst out laughing as Squawky continued, "Awk! Roger! Your Toastie Twinklies are ready, sweetie pie!"

"I don't have to listen to this!" Roger

said, gruffly, grabbing his backpack and swinging it over his shoulders. The backpack was upside down, and all his books spilled out, along with a couple of feathers. The kids stopped laughing and stared as Patti folded her arms and said, "Hah! You were saying?"

"All right! All right, I admit it!" Roger blurted out. He looked guiltily at Ms. Kristal. "I'm sorry, Ms. Kristal. I didn't mean to upset you. I was going to bring Squawky back before you noticed he was gone, but I couldn't get him to cooperate. I just wanted to teach him to say things like, 'Roger is cool!' and 'Roger rules!' But that crazy bird only copied my mother."

Ms. Kristal smiled at Roger. "I forgive you, Roger," she said. "But I hope you learned a lesson. 'What's done in secret will be shouted from the housetops.'"

Roger grimaced. "Yeah, and from the birdcage!"